What Are Literature Pockets?

In *Literature Pockets—Folktales and Fairy Tales*, seven ... hrough fun, exciting projects. The activities for each story are ... ade from construction paper. (See directions below.) Add the cha... pockets together to make a personalized Folktales and Fairy Tales book for each student to enjoy.

How to Make the Pockets

1. Use a 12″ x 18″ (30.5 x 45.5 cm) piece of construction paper for each pocket. Fold up 6″ (15 cm) to make a 12″ (30.5 cm) square.
2. Staple the right side of the pocket closed.
3. Punch two or three holes in the left side of the pocket.

How to Make the Cover

1. Reproduce the cover illustration on page 3 for each student.
2. Have students color and cut out the illustration and glue it onto a 12″ (30.5 cm) square piece of construction paper to make the cover.
3. Punch two or three holes in the left side of the cover.
4. Fasten the cover and the pockets together. You might use string, ribbon, twine, raffia, or metal rings.

How to Use Literature Pockets
Folktales and Fairy Tales

Step 1

Assemble a blank pocket book for each student. (See page 1.)

Step 2

Choose the first story you want to study. Reproduce the pocket label/bookmark page for students. Have students color and cut out the label and glue it onto the first pocket in their book.

Step 3

Complete the pocket.

- Have students color and cut out the bookmark and glue it onto a 4½" x 12" (11.5 x 30.5 cm) strip of construction paper. Have them use the bookmark to preview and review the story characters.

- Reproduce and assemble a minibook for each student. Read the story with students. Have them use the edge of their bookmark to track the text.

- Have students do the follow-up activities and place the paperwork in the pocket with their bookmark and story.

Note: Reproduce this cover illustration for students to color, cut out, and glue onto the cover of their Folktales and Fairy Tales book.

Folktales and Fairy Tales

Name ____________________

The Little Red Hen

Pocket Label and Bookmark..................... page 5
Have students use these reproducibles to make The Little Red Hen pocket label and bookmark. (See page 2.)

The Story of The Little Red Hen.......... pages 6–10
Share and discuss this story of a little red hen who makes bread all by herself when no other animals will help her. Reproduce the story on pages 7–10 for students. Use the teaching ideas on page 6 to preview, read, and review the story. Follow up with the "More to Explore" activities.

A Book of Barnyard Animals............ pages 11–14
Moo. Quack. Cock-a-doodle-doo. Students practice making barnyard sounds as they create a minibook of words from the story.

Sequence the Story................................. page 15
Work with students to sequence these steps for making wheat bread. Have students glue the sentence strips onto the bread slice as the order of each step is identified.

Fields of Wheat....................................... page 16
Use this simple printing project to create fields of golden wheat to display around the classroom. When the display comes down, place the prints in the pockets.

A Little Red Hen .... page 17
Students will love coloring and pasting these simple shapes to make a picture of the little red hen. Have students paste the hen onto construction paper or onto the wheat field made in the previous activity. Extend the activity by having students write or dictate a sentence about the little red hen.

The Little Red Hen

Story characters:

Little Red Hen

Pig

Horse

Cow

Duck

Sheep

Rooster

I liked this story:

- ☐ Yes
- ☐ No

This bookmark belongs to

____

(your name)

Share The Little Red Hen

Preview the Story

State the title of the story, and have students read aloud the names of the characters listed on the bookmark. Distribute copies of the story (pages 7–10), and have students preview the first three pictures. Invite students who are unfamiliar with the story to predict where the story takes place and tell what the little red hen is doing and why.

Read the Story

Read the story aloud as students follow along. Have students track the text and underline or frame key words. Encourage them to chime in with the repeated response, "Not I. Good-bye." Point out picture clues and context clues that help explain parts of the story. After you have read the story aloud, encourage students to reread the story independently or with a partner.

Review the Story

Discuss the characters, setting, and plot of the story. Ask questions such as the following to help students recall the sequence of events, draw conclusions, and share opinions:

- Why did the little red hen grow and gather wheat?
- Who did she ask for help? What did they all say?
- How do you know that the little red hen was a hard worker?
- Why did the little red hen eat all the bread herself?
- What lesson did you learn from the story?
- What would you do if someone asked you for help?

More to Explore

- Find the Rhymes

  Work with students to find each pair of rhyming words in the story. Then reread the story aloud, and have students chime in with the correct rhyming words.

- Compare and Contrast Different Versions

  Read aloud another version of "The Little Red Hen." Work with students to compare and contrast the two versions, using a Venn diagram or a comparison chart.

The Little Red Hen 1	Both Versions	The Little Red Hen 2
• Has five other characters—pig, horse, cow, sheep, rooster. • The little red hen asks six different animals to help her. • The little red hen eats the bread all by herself.	• The little red hen and the duck are in both stories. • The little red hen makes wheat bread, starting with planting the seeds.	• Has one other main character—a goose. • The little red hen asks a duck and a goose to help again and again. • The little red hen and her chicks eat the bread.

So the little red hen planted it herself.

2

It grew!
Yahoo!
Who will help me cut it?
Not I.
Good-bye.
So the little red hen cut it herself.
3

I cut the wheat.
Now, I repeat.
Who will help me thresh it?
Not I.
Good-bye.
So the little red hen threshed it herself.
4

So the little red hen ground it herself.

5

So the little red hen kneaded it herself.

6

So the little red hen baked it herself. **7**

And the little red hen ate it herself! **8**

A Book of Barnyard Animals

Materials

- pages 12–14, reproduced for students
- overhead transparencies of pages 12–14, cut apart
- overhead projector
- scissors
- glue
- crayons
- stapler

Steps to Follow

1. Distribute the reproduced pages. Ask students to trace over each animal name. Then have them cut apart the animal cards and the sound strips.
2. Project the transparencies of the animal cards, one at a time. Ask students to name the animal shown.
3. Say the animal sound and have students repeat it as they look for the matching sound strip. Project the sound-strip transparency to confirm the correct choice.
4. Have students glue the sound strip into the box below the animal. Students will need to fold "cock-a-doodle-doo" in half, gluing only the right half into the box.
5. Invite students to color the animal cards after they attach all the sound strips.
6. Have students staple the cards together to make a book. Students may staple the cards alphabetically or in the order by which the animals appear in the story.

Animal Cards

Barnyard Animals

(your name)

duck

paste

sheep

paste

rooster

paste

Animal Cards

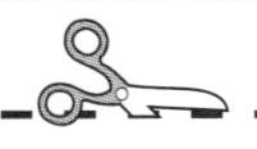

hen

paste

cow

paste

pig

paste

horse

paste

Animal Sound Strips

cluck	moo
grunt	quack
neigh	baa

cock-a-doodle-doo

fold

cluck	moo
grunt	quack
neigh	baa

cock-a-doodle-doo

fold

Note: Reproduce this page for each student. Use the directions on page 4 to help students complete the activity.

Sequence the Story

Bake the bread.

Make the dough.

Plant the wheat.

Thresh the wheat.

Cut the wheat.

Grind the wheat.

Fields of Wheat

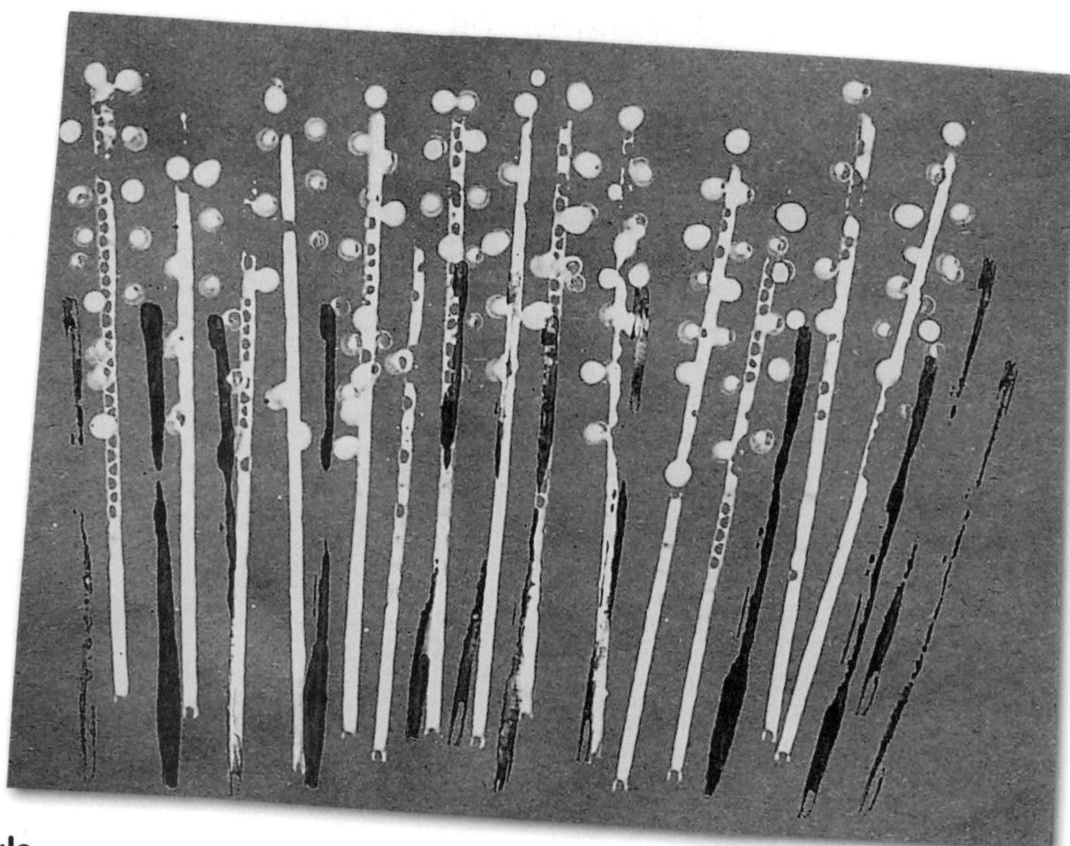

Materials

- newspaper
- paper plates
- yellow tempera paint
- strips of cardboard
- pencils with new erasers
- brown construction paper

Steps to Follow

1. Cover the work areas with newspaper. Put out paper plates containing a small amount of tempera paint.
2. Demonstrate how to press-print a stalk of wheat by using the edge of the cardboard to make the stem and using the eraser tip to make the wheat seeds.
3. Have each student create a field of wheat by making a series of stalks across their paper and then adding the wheat seeds.
4. Display the "wheat fields" around the classroom before having students place them in their pockets.
5. The prints may also be used as a backing for the cut-and-paste hen that students will be making in the next activity.

Note: Reproduce this page for each student. Use the directions on page 4 to help students complete the activity.

A Little Red Hen

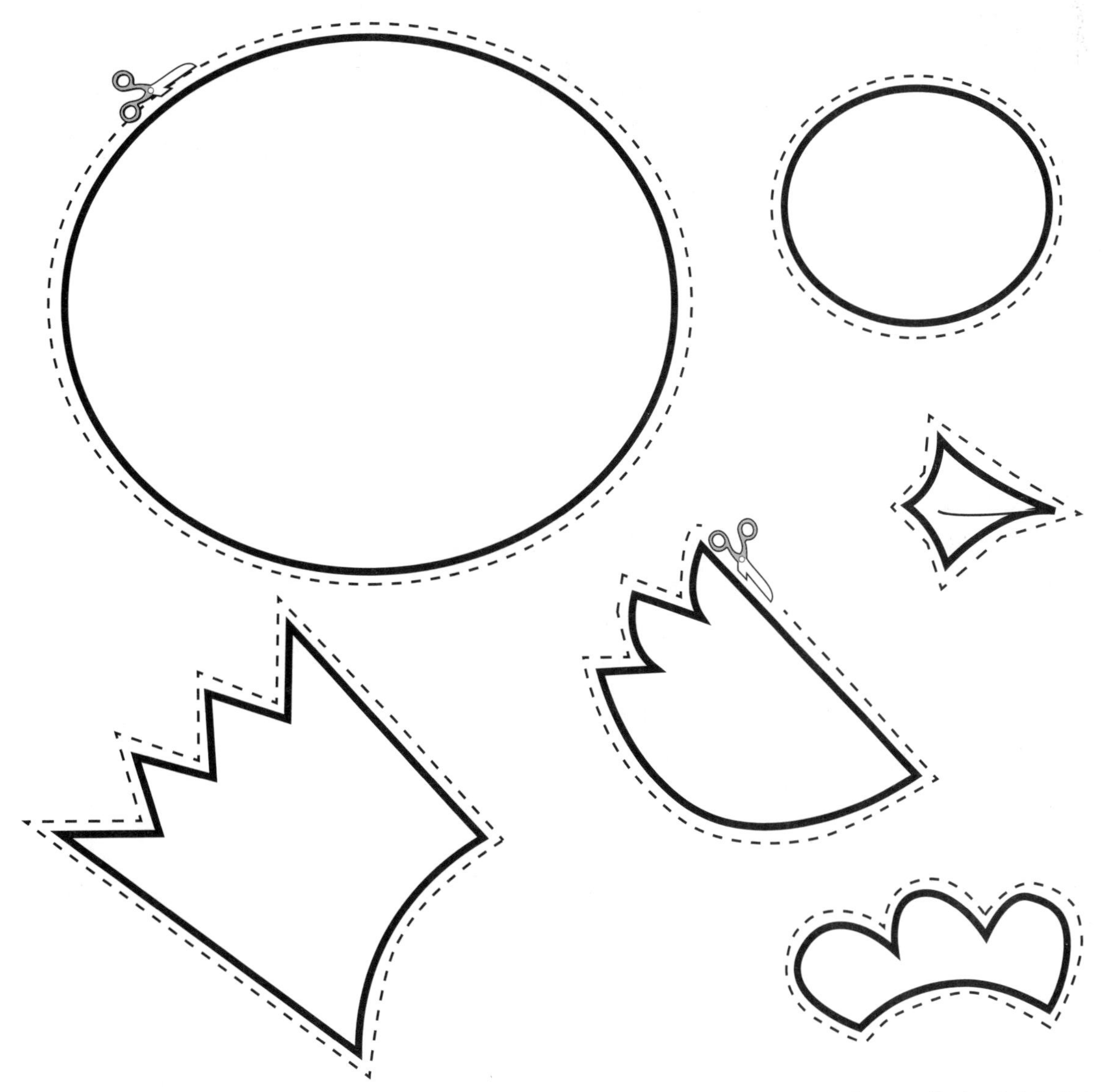

The Three Little Pigs

Pocket Label and Bookmark....................page 19
Have students use these reproducibles to make The Three Little Pigs pocket label and bookmark. (See page 2.)

The Story of The Three Little Pigs.... pages 20–25
Share and discuss this story of three little pigs who try to keep a hungry wolf from entering their homes. Reproduce the story on pages 21–25 for students. Use the teaching ideas on page 20 to preview, read, and review the story. Follow up with the "More to Explore" activities.

My Three Little Pigs Word Book............. page 26
Students trace words, color pictures, and cut pages apart to make a minibook of words from the story. Assemble the books by punching a hole in the top left corner and tying the pages together with yarn.

Sequence the Story................................ page 27
Have students color and cut out these sequence cards and glue them in order onto a 4" x 18" (10 x 45.5 cm) strip of construction paper. Fold the strip in half to fit it in the pocket.

One Little Pig.. page 28
With a few shapes and some colorful details, students create their own little pigs. Have students glue their pig onto a sheet of construction paper. Extend the activity by having students write or dictate words or phrases that describe their pig.

My House .... page 29
Students use their imagination to draw and describe a house they would build. Remind students of the materials that the three pigs used to build their homes, and work with students to brainstorm a list of other possible building materials.

The Three Little Pigs

Story characters:

First Little Pig

Second Little Pig

Third Little Pig

Wolf

I liked this story:

☐ Yes

☐ No

This bookmark belongs to

____

(your name)

Share The Three Little Pigs

Preview the Story

State the title of the story, and have students read aloud the names of the characters listed on the bookmark. Distribute copies of the story (pages 21–25), and have students preview the first five pictures. Invite students who are unfamiliar with the story to predict what happens to the three little pigs.

Read the Story

Read the story aloud as students follow along. Have students track the text and underline or frame key words. Point out picture clues and context clues that help explain parts of the story. After you have read the story aloud, encourage students to reread the story independently or with a partner.

Review the Story

Discuss the characters, setting, and plot of the story. Ask questions such as the following to help students recall the sequence of events, identify important details, and share opinions:

- What did the pigs use for building their houses?
- Why did the wolf want to get the little pigs?
- Was the straw house a good idea? Why or why not?
- What did the wolf do after he blew down the straw house?
- Which house was the best? Why?
- What happened at the end of the story?

More to Explore

- Ordinal Numbers

  Explain to students that the words *first, second,* and *third* tell the order of things, such as the order of pigs or the order of men with carts. Invite three students to stand in a line. Ask, "Who's first? Who's second? Who's third?"

- "Noisy" Words

  Point out the "noisy" words used to describe how the wolf knocks on each door. Ask students which words describe a quiet knock and which words describe a loud knock. Then invite them to demonstrate the different knocks on their desks.

- Repeat the Refrain

  Divide the class into two groups, the "wolves" and "pigs." As you reread the story aloud, have the wolves chime in with their repeated refrain, and have the pigs chime in with theirs. Then have the groups switch roles, and read the story again.

- Compare and Contrast Different Versions

  Read aloud another version of "The Three Little Pigs." Work with students to compare and contrast the two versions, using a Venn diagram or a comparison chart.

The Three Little Pigs
1

The three little pigs wanted to build new houses.
They found a cart full of straw.
They found a cart full of bricks.
They found a cart full of sticks.
2

The first little pig built a straw house.
The second little pig built a stick house.
The third little pig built a brick house.

3

A big bad wolf saw the three little pigs.
He wanted pig stew for lunch!
He went to the straw house.

Tap, tap, tap.
"Little pig, little pig, let me come in."

The first little pig saw the wolf.
"No, no, big bad wolf, I won't let you in.
Not by the hair on my chinny chin chin."

4

The wolf shouted, “Then I’ll huff and I’ll puff and I’ll blow your house down!” So he huffed and he puffed and he blew the house down.

“Oh no!” cried the first little pig. He ran to the second little pig’s house.

5

The mad, hungry wolf followed the pig to the stick house.

Bang, bang, bang!
“Little pig, little pig, let me come in.”

The second little pig saw the wolf.
“No, no, big bad wolf, I won’t let you in.
Not by the hair on my chinny chin chin.”

6

The wolf shouted, "Then I'll huff and I'll puff and I'll blow your house down!" So he huffed and he puffed and he blew the house down.

"Oh no!" cried the two little pigs. They ran to the third little pig's house.

7

The mad, hungry, tired wolf followed the pigs to the brick house.

Pound, pound, pound!
"Little pig, little pig, let me come in!"

The third little pig saw the wolf.
"No, no, big bad wolf, I won't let you in.
Not by the hair on my chinny chin chin."

8

The wolf shouted, "Then I'll huff and I'll puff and I'll blow your house down!"
So he huffed and he puffed.
But the house was too strong.
He huffed and puffed again.
But he could not blow the house down.

9

The wolf yelled, "I will find another way!"
He climbed down the chimney.
But there was a fire at the bottom.
"Ouch!" he cried.
He jumped out of the chimney and ran into the woods.
He never came back again.

10

Note: Reproduce this page for each student. Use the directions on page 18 to help students complete the activity.

My Three Little Pigs Word Book

My
Three Little Pigs
Word Book

____
(your name)

sticks

pig

straw

wolf

bricks

Note: Reproduce this page for each student. Use the directions on page 18 to help students complete the activity.

Sequence the Story

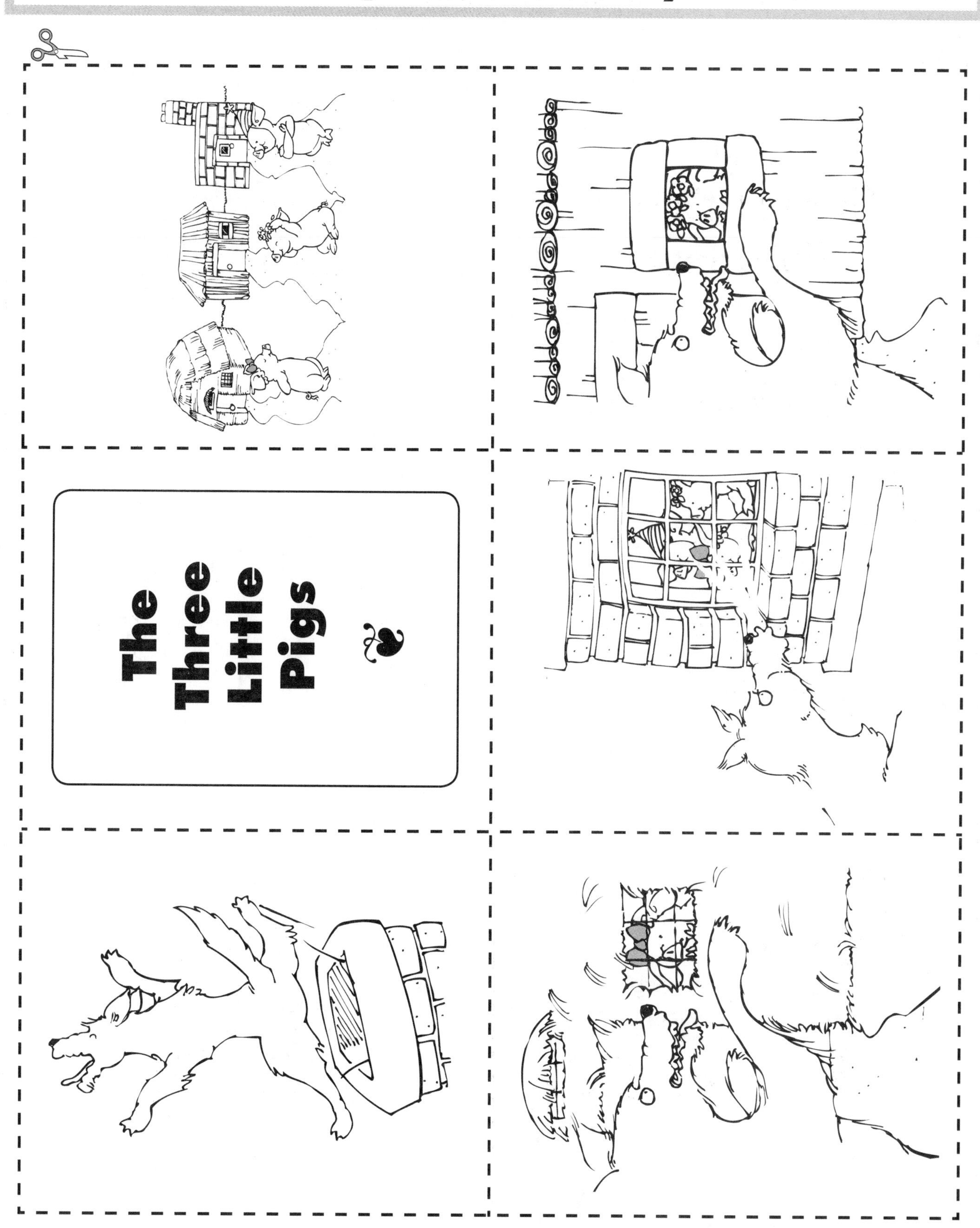

Note: Reproduce this page for each student. Use the directions on page 18 to help students complete the activity.

One Little Pig

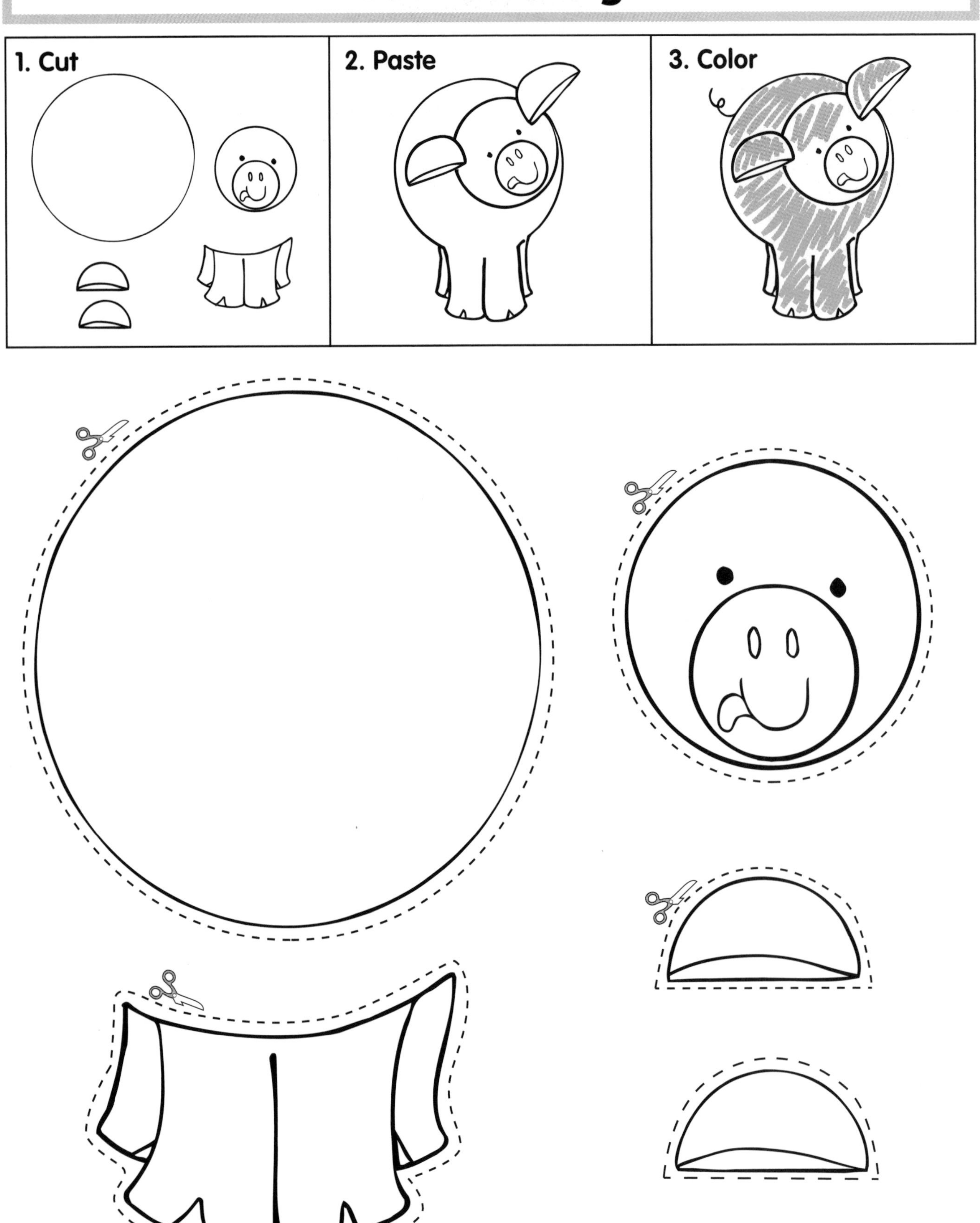

Note: Reproduce this page for each student. Use the directions on page 18 to help students complete the activity.

Name: ______________________________

My House

I built a house of ______________________________.

It looked like this.

Goldilocks and the Three Bears

Pocket Label and Bookmark.................... page 31
Have students use these reproducibles to make the Goldilocks and the Three Bears pocket label and bookmark. (See page 2.)

The Story of Goldilocks and the Three Bears.............................. pages 32–36
Share and discuss this story of a curious girl who discovers the home of three bears. Reproduce the story on pages 33–36 for students. Use the teaching ideas on page 32 to preview, read, and review the story. Follow up with the "More to Explore" activities.

Peekaboo Clues .... pages 37 and 38
Learning becomes a game of "peekaboo" with this illustrated flap book of questions and answers.

The Three Bears' House............ pages 39 and 40
Students pull characters out of a paper-bag house as they retell what happens to Goldilocks.

Do You Like Porridge?............................. page 41
Students become connoisseurs of porridge as they taste and evaluate instant oatmeal.

Grocery-Bag Bears .... page 42
Wrinkled paper bags are the perfect material to make "furry" bears. Have students display their critters as they tell a new story about the three bears.

Goldilocks and the Three Bears

Story characters:

Goldilocks

Papa Bear

Mama Bear

Baby Bear

I liked this story:

☐ Yes

☐ No

This bookmark belongs to

____

(your name)

Share Goldilocks and the Three Bears

Preview the Story

State the title of the story, and have students read aloud the names of the characters listed on the bookmark. Distribute copies of the story (pages 33–36), and have students preview the first three pictures. Invite students who are unfamiliar with the story to predict what happens to Goldilocks.

Read the Story

Read the story aloud as students follow along. Have students track the text and underline or frame key words. Point out picture clues and context clues that help explain parts of the story. After you have read the story aloud, encourage students to reread the story independently or with a partner.

Review the Story

Discuss the characters, setting, and plot of the story. Ask questions such as the following to help students recall important details, share opinions, and make judgments:

- Why do you think Goldilocks went into the bears' house?
- What did Goldilocks do in the house? Do you think she felt bad about breaking the chair?
- Which bear had the smallest things?
- What happened when the bears came home?
- How do you think Goldilocks felt when she saw the bears?
- What do you think Goldilocks should have done when she got to the house?
- How can the bears keep their house safe?

More to Explore

- Rhythm and Rhyme

  Reread the story aloud, page by page, and work with students to find the rhyming words. Then reread the story again, sentence by sentence, and have students repeat after you. Encourage them to tap out the rhythm of the verses and emphasize the rhyming words.

- Sizes, Shapes, and Textures

  Have students compare and contrast the bears' chairs, bowls, and beds. Encourage them to think of a variety of words that could be used to describe those objects, such as *large/small*, *hard/soft*, *hot/cold*, and *lumpy/smooth*.

- Compare and Contrast Different Versions

  Read aloud another version of "Goldilocks and the Three Bears." Work with students to compare and contrast the two versions, using a Venn diagram or a comparison chart.

Three bears left their forest home,
To take a little walk.
But Papa and Mama and Baby Bear
Left the door unlocked.

A small girl found the three bears' home.
The door was open wide.
"There's no one here," said Goldilocks.
"I think I'll go inside."

3

She saw three chairs inside the house.
She tried them, one by one.
The last one broke when she sat down.
"Well, this is not much fun!"

4

She saw three bowls of tasty porridge.
"I think I'll have a bite."
She tried the first and then the second.
The last one was just right!

5

Now Goldilocks was full and tired.
She wanted a place to rest.
She saw a row of cozy beds.
The small one was the best.

6

She did not hear the bears return.
They saw the open door.
"Who's been inside?" asked Baby Bear.
"Look! Footprints on the floor!"

7

"Who broke my chair? Who ate my food?"
The bears looked all around.
"Come over here," yelled Baby Bear,
"And see what I just found!"

The girl woke up. She saw the bears.
She raced right out the door.
When she got home, she told her mom,
"I'll never go there anymore."

8

Peekaboo Clues

Materials

- page 38, reproduced for each student
- 9" x 12" (23 x 30.5 cm) construction paper
- scissors
- glue
- crayons

Steps to Follow

❶ Guide students through the following steps to make a "peekaboo" flap book of questions and answers:

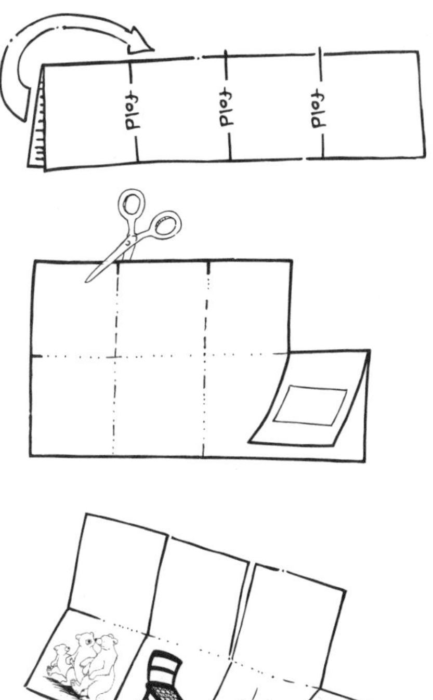

a. Fold the construction paper in half lengthwise.

b. Fold the paper crosswise in half, then in half again to make four sections.

c. Open the paper and cut on the fold lines from one edge to the center fold as shown.

d. Cut apart the questions and pictures for the flap book.

e. Fold down the flaps one at a time. Paste a question on the flap. Paste the correct picture under the flap.

f. Color the pictures.

❷ Read aloud each question with students. Have them flip open the flap and read the correct answer.

Peekaboo Clues

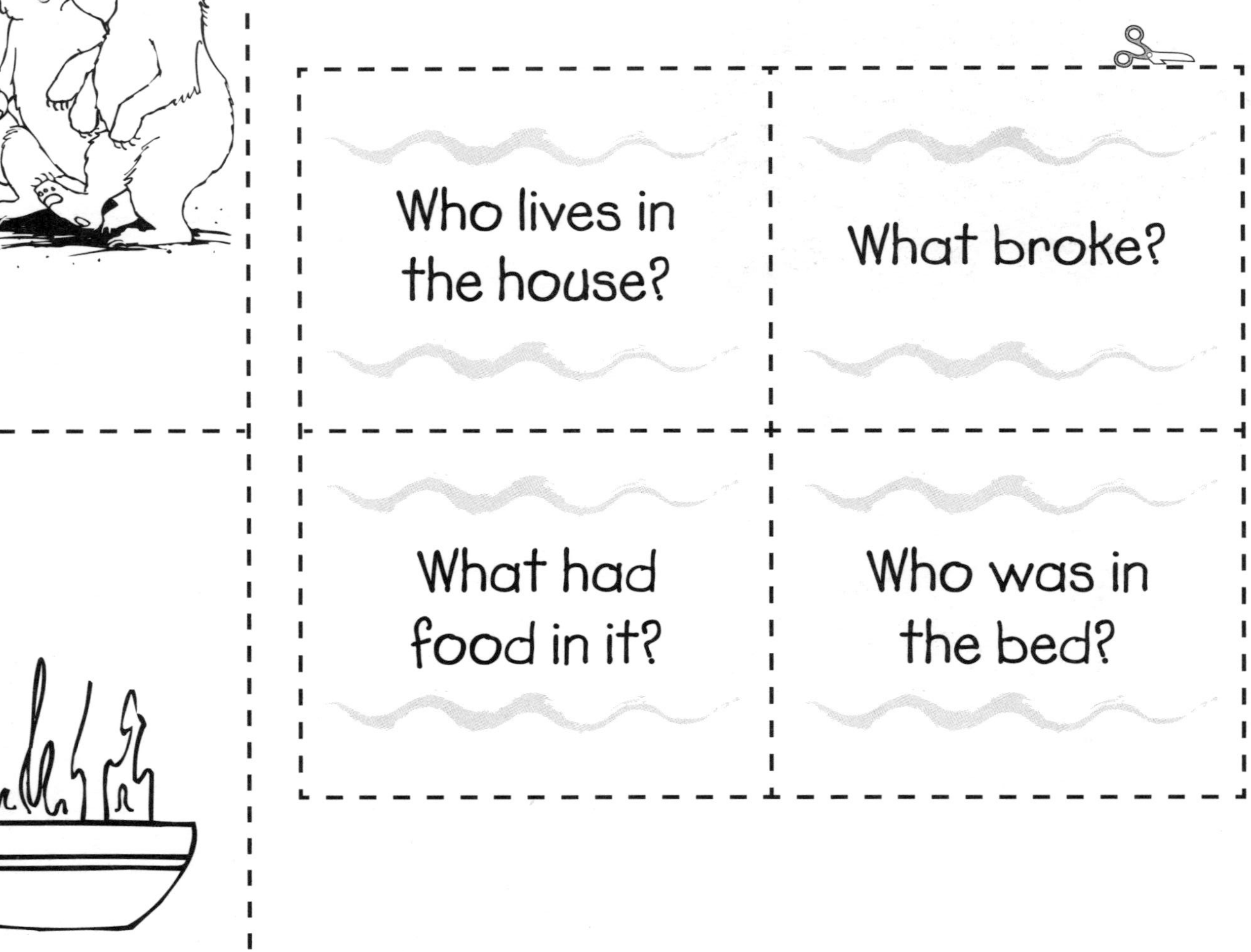

bowl

The Three Bears' House

Materials

- page 40, reproduced for each student
- paper lunch bag for each student
- scissors
- paper scraps
- glue
- crayons

Steps to Follow

1. Guide students through the following steps to make a paper-bag house. In advance, draw dotted lines on the bags to show students where to cut the roof.

   a. Cut the top of the bag to make a pointed roof.

   b. Use the paper scraps to make the door, windows, and other parts of the house. Glue the parts onto the bag.

   c. Draw details to finish the house.

2. After students finish the house, have them color and cut out the characters. Show students how to fold the characters along the fold line to stand them up.

3. Invite more advanced students to make paper furniture and other objects for the bears' house, including chairs, beds, and bowls of porridge.

4. Have students place the paper characters and objects inside the house.

5. Invite students to use their paper-bag houses, characters, and objects to retell the story "Goldilocks and the Three Bears."

   Note: Flatten the house and the cutouts to fit them in the pocket.

Character Patterns

Do You Like Porridge?

Materials

- porridge survey form (below), reproduced for each student
- ingredients to make instant oatmeal
- paper bowls and plastic spoons
- scissors
- glue
- 6″ x 8″ (15 x 20 cm) construction paper

Steps to Follow

1. Prepare the instant oatmeal in advance or with students. (Be certain that no students are allergic to any of the ingredients.)
2. Distribute bowls of oatmeal and have a tasting party.
3. Ask students to complete their porridge survey form. Have them write "like" or "do not like" on the line.
4. Have students cut out the paper bowl and glue it onto construction paper. Then have them cut it out again, leaving a slight border.

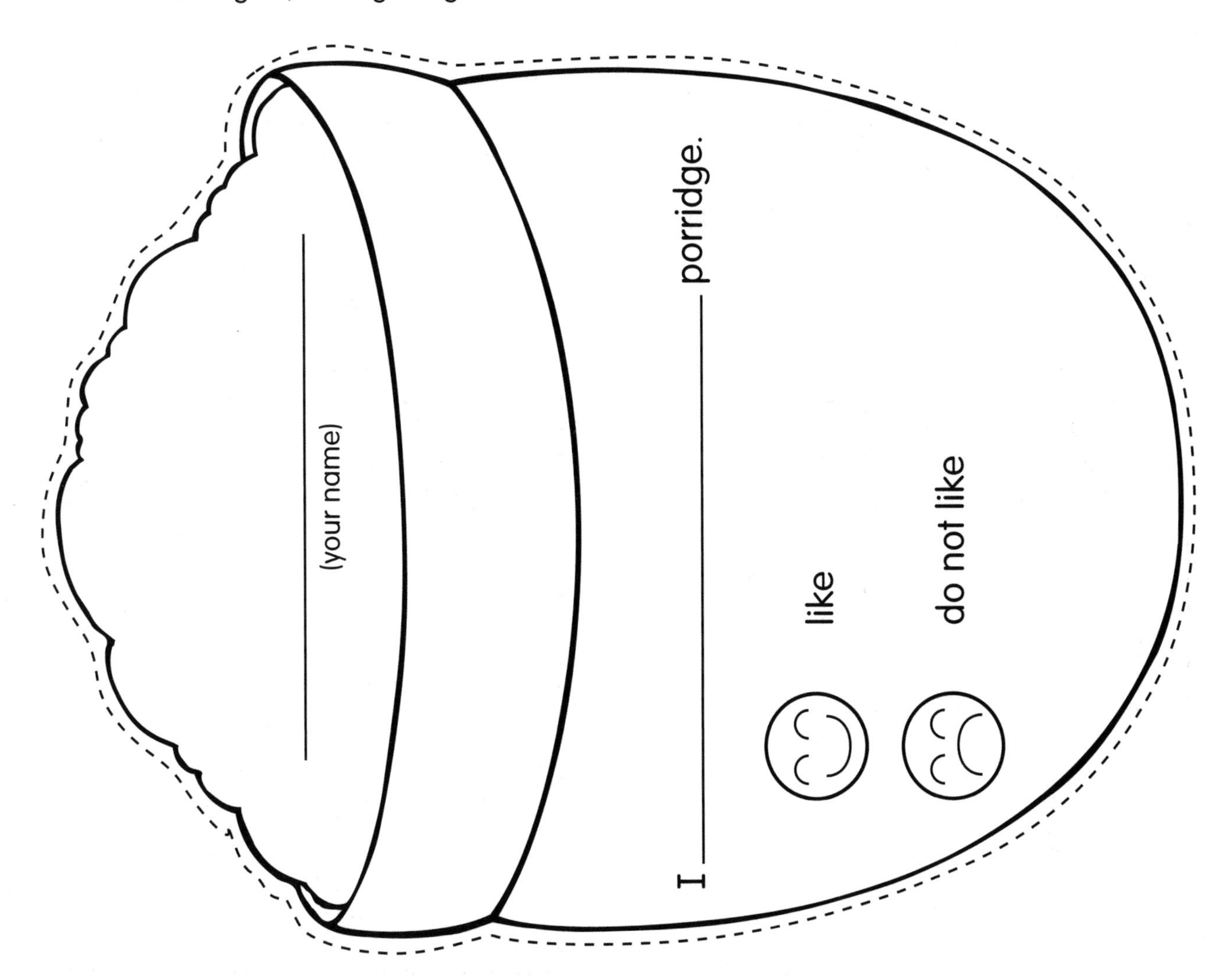

Grocery-Bag Bears

Materials

- 1 lunch-size brown grocery bag
- 9" x 12" (23 x 30.5 cm) brightly colored construction paper
- crayons
- scissors
- glue

Steps to Follow

1. Ask students to crumple the brown paper and smooth it out. This gives a "furry" look to the bear.
2. Have students cut the bag as shown.
3. Glue the bear parts to the construction paper.
4. Have students add details to their bear with crayon.

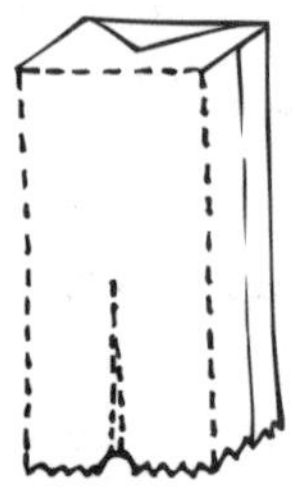

front of bag

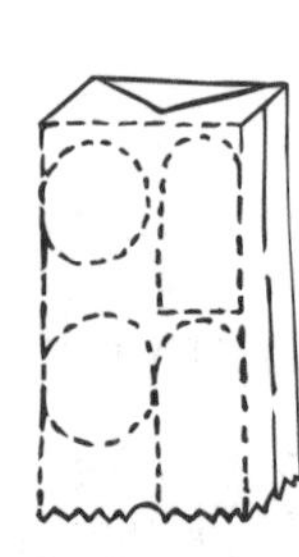

back of bag

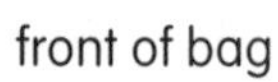

5. Extend the activity by having groups of three students make up a new story about the three bears. Have them hold up their bears as they tell the story. Students may tell what the three bears did after Goldilocks left the house.

The Gingerbread Man

Pocket Label and Bookmark...................page 44
Have students use these reproducibles to make The Gingerbread Man pocket label and bookmark. (See page 2.)

The Story of
The Gingerbread Man.....................pages 45–49
Share and discuss this story of a runaway cookie. Reproduce the story on pages 46–49 for students. Use the teaching ideas on page 45 to preview, read, and review the story. Follow up with the "More to Explore" activities.

The Gingerbread Man
Word Book.................................pages 50 and 51
Students color, cut, and fold this reproducible sheet to create a miniature "poof" book of words from the story.

Sequence the Story................................page 52
Have students color and cut out these sequence cards and glue them in order onto a 4" x 18" (10 x 45.5 cm) strip of construction paper. Fold the strip in half to fit it in the pocket.

A Gingerbread Man Puppet......pages 53 and 54
This animated stick puppet with movable arms and "running" feet will delight students. Have them make the puppet and use it to retell the story.

It Rhymes...page 55
Students learn rhyming words as they color a picture of the gingerbread man. Remind students of the rhyming words from the story refrain. (*can, man*) Then read the rhyming words on the picture with students. Guide them in coloring each set of rhyming parts. Extend the activity by having students list other rhyming words for *man*, *run*, and *cat*.

The Gingerbread Man

Story characters:

Gingerbread Man

Little Old Woman

Little Old Man

Dog

Cat

Cow

Horse

Farmer

Fox

I liked this story:

☐ Yes

☐ No

This bookmark belongs to

____

(your name)

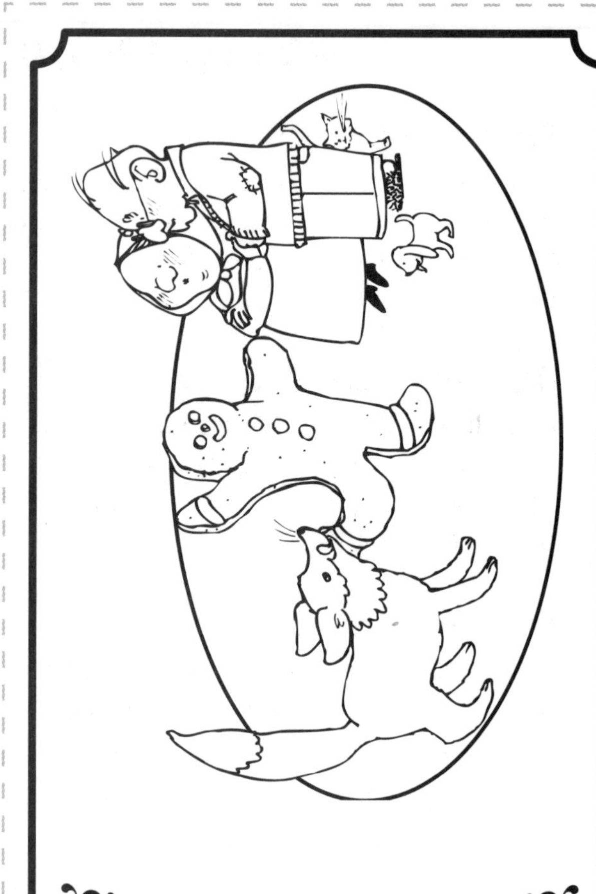

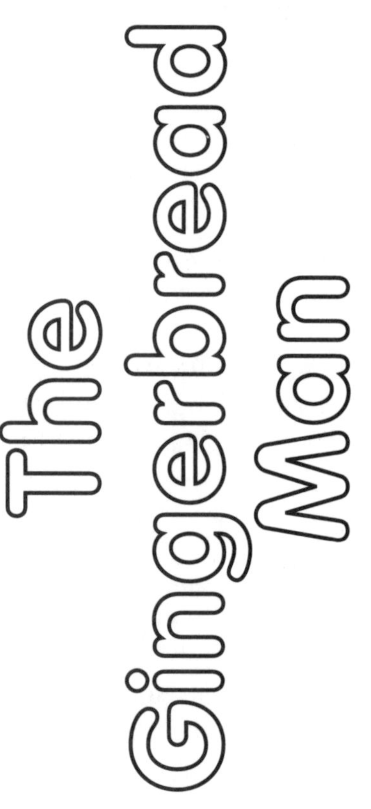

©2002 by Evan-Moor Corp. • EMC 2730

Share The Gingerbread Man

Preview the Story

State the title of the story, and have students read aloud the names of the characters listed on the bookmark. Distribute copies of the story (pages 46–49), and have students preview the first four pictures. Invite students who are unfamiliar with the story to predict what happens to the gingerbread man.

Read the Story

Read the story aloud as students follow along. Have students track the text and underline or frame key words. Point out picture clues and context clues that help explain parts of the story. After you have read the story aloud, encourage students to reread the story independently or with a partner.

Review the Story

Discuss the characters, setting, and plot of the story. Ask questions such as the following to help students recall important details, draw conclusions, and identify problems and solutions:

- How was the gingerbread man different from other cookies?
- How do you know that the gingerbread man was a fast runner?
- Who did the gingerbread man run away from?
- Why did the gingerbread man stop at the river?
- How did the fox trick the gingerbread man?
- If you were the gingerbread man, how would you have crossed the river?

More to Explore

- Gingerbread Men

  Bring in gingerbread men cookies for the class. Reread "The Gingerbread Man" aloud as students enjoy their cookies.

- Expand the Story

  Work with students to write a new page about the gingerbread man running away from other people or animals. Follow the wording used on the fourth or fifth page of the story. Then reread the story and include the new page.

- Compare and Contrast Different Versions

  Read aloud another version of "The Gingerbread Man." Work with students to compare and contrast the two versions, using a Venn diagram or a comparison chart.

Once upon a time there was a little old woman.
She lived in a cottage with her little old husband.
They had a tiny dog and a small cat.

One day the little old woman made a big gingerbread man.

She was surprised when the gingerbread man jumped out of the oven.

Quick as a wink, he ran out the door and down the road.

3

The old woman and old man ran after the gingerbread man.
They could not catch him.

The dog and cat ran after the gingerbread man.
They could not catch him.

He shouted happily,
"Run, run, as fast as you can.
You can't catch me,
I'm the gingerbread man!"

4

The gingerbread man ran on and on.
No one could catch him.

He ran away from a horse and a cow.

He ran away from a farmer picking corn.

He shouted happily,
"Run, run, as fast as you can.
You can't catch me,
I'm the gingerbread man!"

5

The gingerbread man stopped at a wide river.
He could not swim.

Along came a hungry fox.
"I will take you across the river," he said.
"Just jump on my back."

6

The fox went into the river.
He went deeper and deeper into the water.

The gingerbread man hopped up to the fox's head.
Quick as a wink, the fox gobbled him up.

7

The Gingerbread Man Word Book

Materials

- page 51, reproduced for each student
- scissors
- crayons

Steps to Follow

❶ Guide students through the following steps to make a minibook:

a. Fold the paper in half on fold line 1. Open the paper and fold it in half crosswise on fold line 2.

b. Fold it again on fold line 3. Then unfold it to line 2 and cut a slit along the dotted line from the center to the next crosswise fold line.

c. Open the paper and refold it lengthwise in half. Push both sides inward as shown. Fold all the sides together in one direction to create the book. Be sure to fold so the title page is on top.

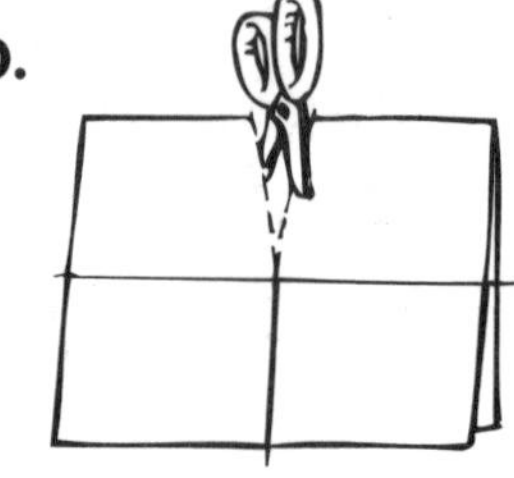

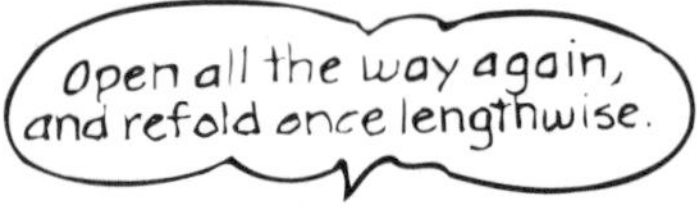

c.

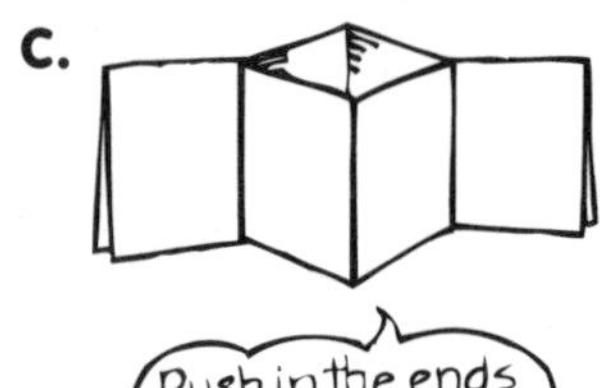

❷ Invite students to color the pictures. Then read the book together.

cut
cut
fold 1
8
The End
fox
7
fold 3
fold 3
1
The Gingerbread Man
farmer
6
fold 2
cut
fold 2
2
old woman and old man
horse and cow
5
fold 3
fold 3
3
gingerbread man
dog and cat
4
fold 1

Note: Reproduce this page for each student. Use the directions on page 43 to help students complete the activity.

Sequence the Story

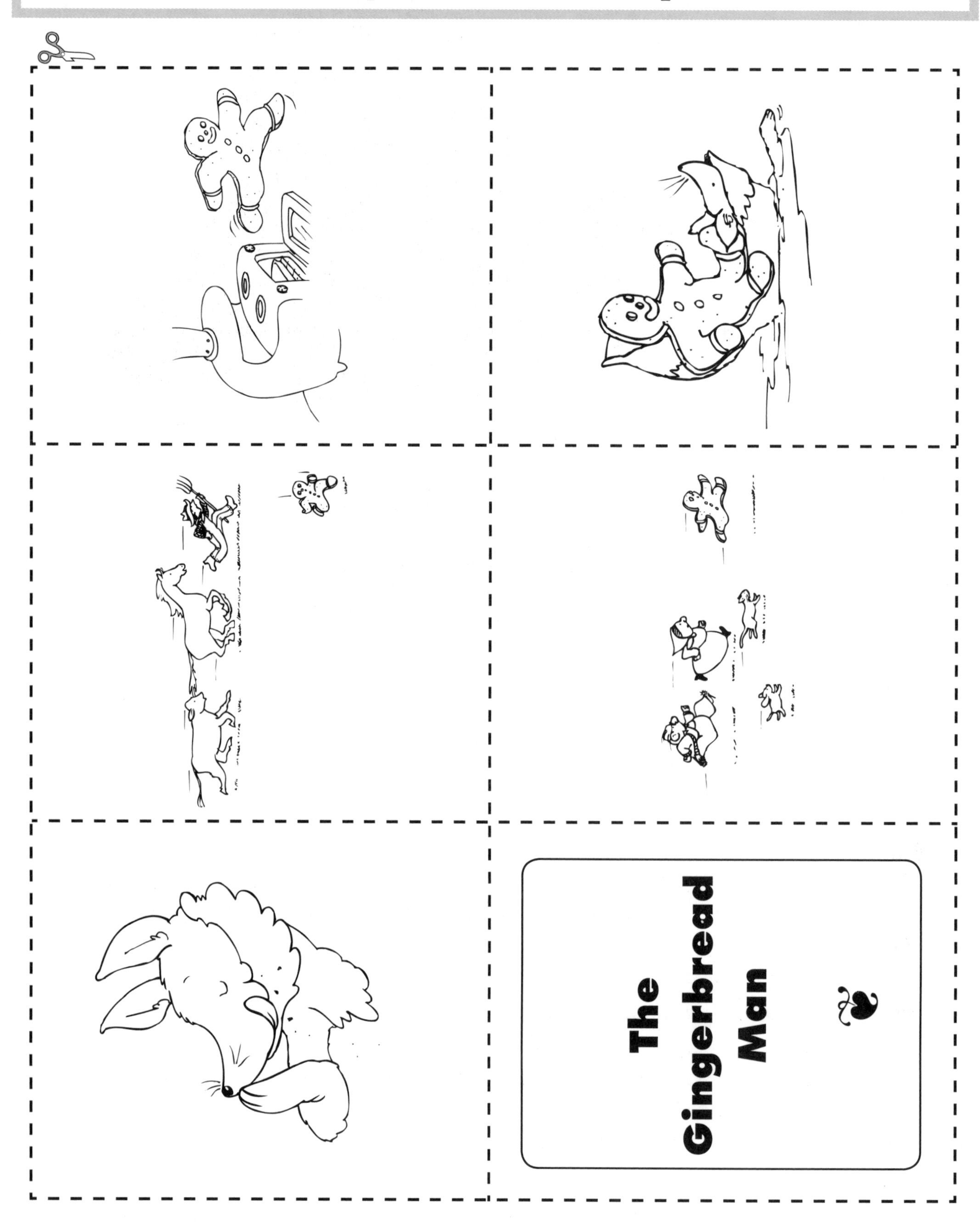

A Gingerbread Man Puppet

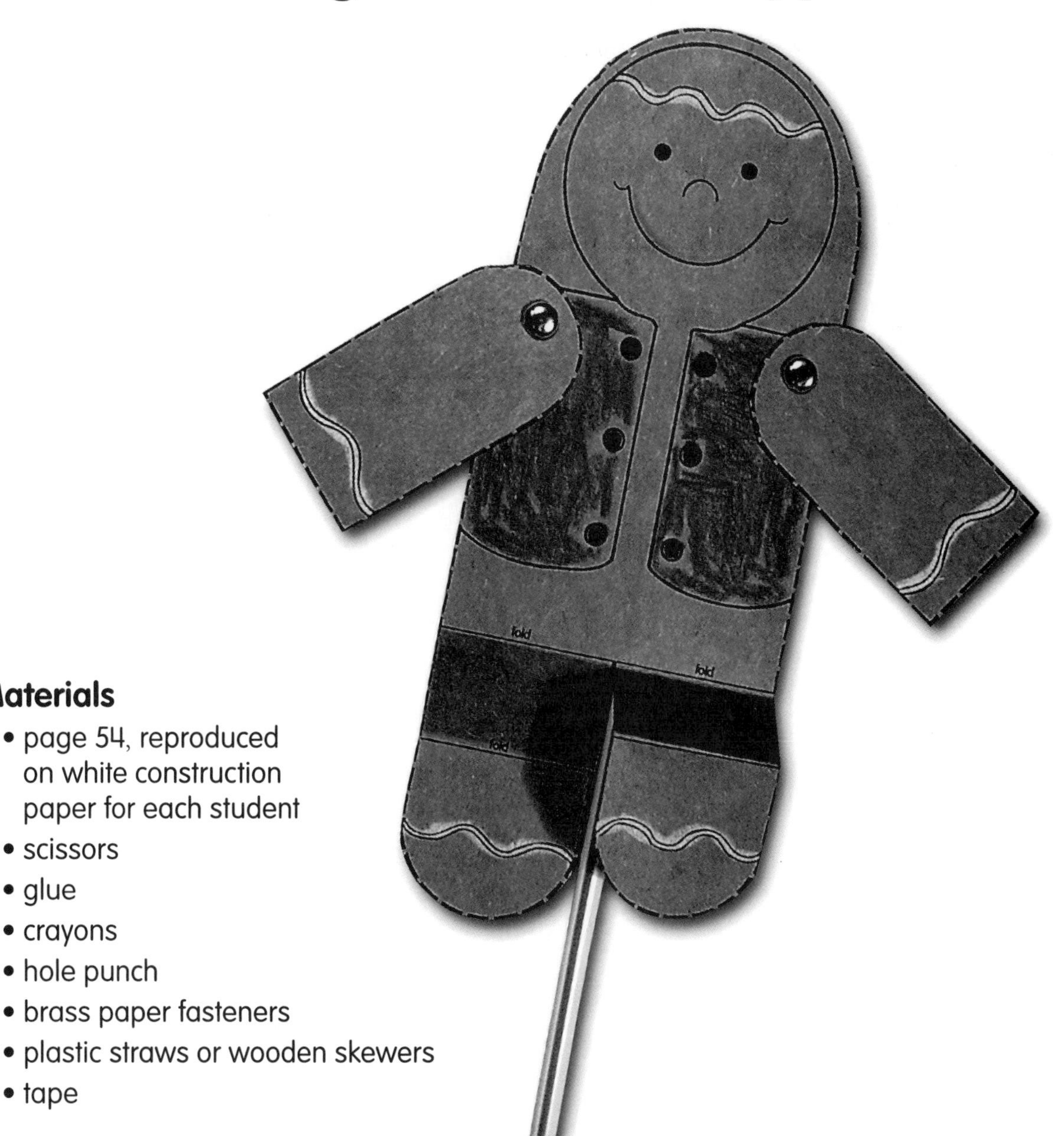

Materials

- page 54, reproduced on white construction paper for each student
- scissors
- glue
- crayons
- hole punch
- brass paper fasteners
- plastic straws or wooden skewers
- tape

Steps to Follow

1. Have students color and cut out the parts of the gingerbread man. As students work, go around the room and punch the holes in the arms and shoulders of the puppets.
2. Show students how to use two paper fasteners to connect the arms to the shoulders. The arms should be attached loosely so they swing freely.
3. Have students fold the legs on the lines to make a "running" puppet.
4. Distribute pieces of tape, and have students attach a straw (or skewer) to the back of the puppet to make a handle. Be sure students position the straw from the head to the waist to keep the puppet from flopping.
5. Invite students to use their puppets to retell the story or recite the refrain.

Puppet Pattern

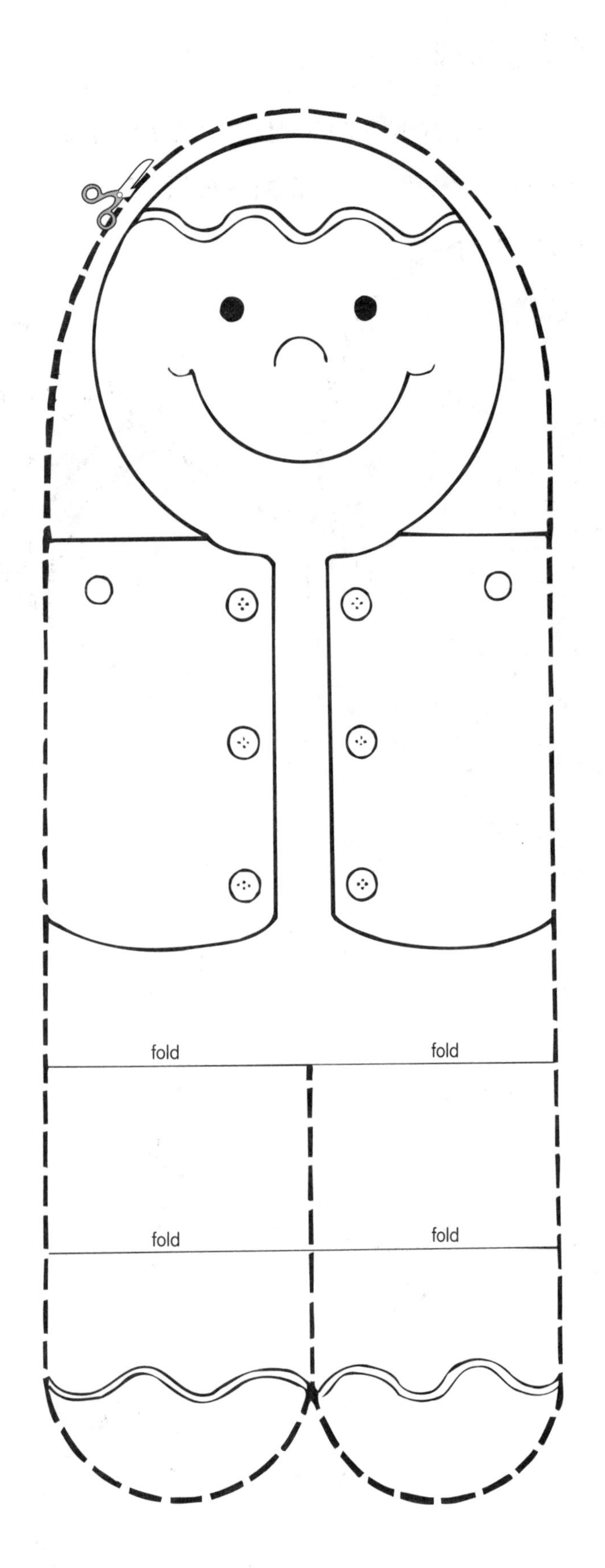

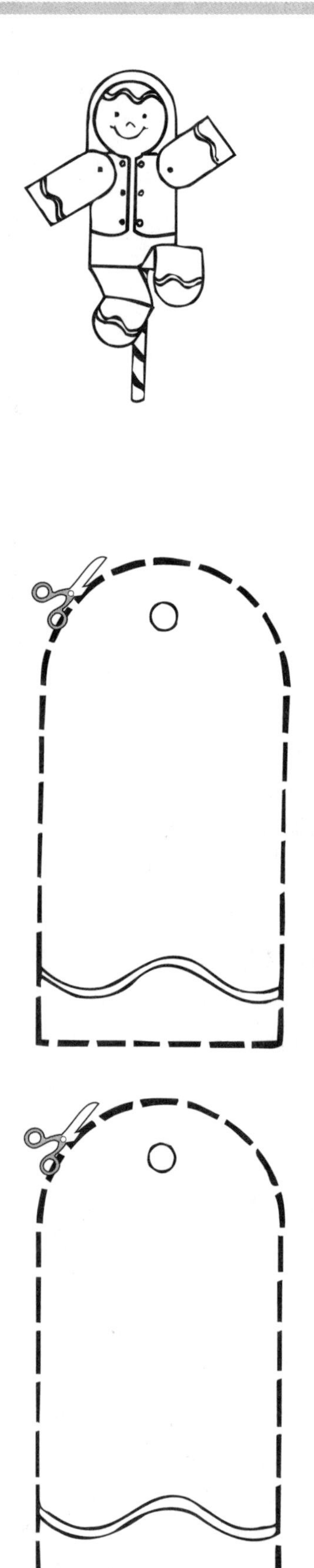

Note: Reproduce this page for each student. Use the directions on page 43 to help students complete the activity.

It Rhymes

Find the parts that rhyme. Use the same color for those parts.

***man*—brown** ***run*—red** ***cat*—blue**

Little Red Riding Hood

Pocket Label and Bookmark................... page 57
Have students use these reproducibles to make the Little Red Riding Hood pocket label and bookmark. (See page 2.)

The Story of Little Red Riding Hood .... pages 58–63
Share and discuss this story of a little girl who meets a hungry wolf on her way to her grandmother's house. Reproduce the story on pages 59–63 for students. Use the teaching ideas on page 58 to preview, read, and review the story. Follow up with the "More to Explore" activities.

Little Red Riding Hood Word Book................................pages 64 and 65
This scenic minibook helps students recall important details as they practice reading new words from the story. Have students trace the words, color the pictures, and staple the pages together. After the book is assembled, have students read the words aloud as they point to the matching pictures.

Sequence the Story................................ page 66
Have students color and cut out these sequence cards and glue them in order onto a 4" x 18" (10 x 45.5 cm) strip of construction paper. Fold the strip in half to fit it in the pocket.

Little Red Riding Hood Puppets .... page 67
Students create a complete set of stick puppets by taping character cutouts onto craft sticks. Students use their puppets to retell the story. Have students store the puppets in an envelope or a resealable plastic bag in the pocket.

A Basket of Goodies for Granny ....pages 68 and 69
This activity promotes thoughtfulness and compassion as students fill a basket with items they would take to a sick grandmother.

Little Red Riding Hood

Story characters:

Little Red Riding Hood

Granny

Mother

Wolf

Hunter

I liked this story:

- ☐ Yes
- ☐ No

This bookmark belongs to

____

(your name)

Share Little Red Riding Hood

Preview the Story

State the title of the story, and have students read aloud the names of the characters listed on the bookmark. Distribute copies of the story (pages 59–63), and have students preview the first four pictures. Invite students who are unfamiliar with the story to predict where the story takes place and tell what happens to the little girl.

Read the Story

Read the story aloud as students follow along. Have students track the text and underline or frame key words. Point out picture clues and context clues that help explain parts of the story. After you have read the story aloud, encourage students to reread the story independently or with a partner.

Review the Story

Discuss the characters, setting, and plot of the story. Ask questions such as the following to help students recall the sequence of events, identify important details, and draw conclusions:

- Why was Little Red Riding Hood going to Granny's house?
- Who did Little Red Riding Hood meet on her way through the woods?
- What did the wolf plan to do?
- How did the hunter know that Little Red Riding Hood needed help?
- What did Little Red Riding Hood do that got her into trouble?
- What lesson did Little Red Riding Hood learn?

More to Explore

- Nicknames

  Ask students how the little girl in the story got her nickname. Then invite volunteers to share their nicknames and explain how they got them.

- Action Words

  Work with students to find action words in the story. Demonstrate their meanings if needed. Then invite students to pantomime the actions as you reread the story aloud.

- Compare and Contrast Different Versions

  Read aloud another version of "Little Red Riding Hood." Work with students to compare and contrast the two versions, using a Venn diagram or a comparison chart.

There once was a happy little girl who lived by the woods.
She loved to pick flowers and listen to the birds sing.
She wore a red cape with a little red hood.
She was called Little Red Riding Hood.

2

Little Red Riding Hood's mother gave her a basket.
"Take these goodies to Granny," she said.
"Don't stop along the way. Don't talk to strangers.
Be careful in the woods."

3

Little Red Riding Hood took the basket.
She skipped along the path to Granny's house.

Suddenly a big wolf stepped out from behind a tree.
"Where are you going, little girl?" he asked.

4

"I'm taking these goodies to Granny. She is sick," said Little Red Riding Hood.

"You better hurry," said the wolf. "It's getting late." The wolf watched Little Red Riding Hood leave. Then he ran ahead to Granny's house.

5

The wolf knocked on the door.
When Granny opened the door, he grabbed her.
He locked Granny in the closet.
He put on her nightgown and climbed into her bed.

6

Soon Little Red Riding Hood knocked on the door.
"Granny, I have some goodies for you."

"Come in, my dear. I'm in my bed," called the wolf in Granny's voice.

7

Little Red Riding Hood went to Granny's bed.
She saw the wolf's big eyes and big ears.
She saw his big white teeth.

"Oh, Granny, what big eyes and ears you have!" she said.
"And what big teeth you have, too."

8

"The better to see and hear you with,
my dear," said the wolf.
"And the better to EAT YOU with!"
he growled.

The wolf jumped out of bed.
He grabbed Little Red Riding Hood.
She began to scream.

9

A hunter heard Little Red Riding Hood.
He rushed to Granny's house and caught the wolf.
He let Granny out of the closet.
He took Little Red Riding Hood home.

10

Note: Reproduce pages 64 and 65 for each student. Use the directions on page 56 to help students complete the activity.

Little Red Riding Hood Word Book

Red Riding Hood

wolf

hunter

Granny

Little Red Riding Hood Word Book

bowl

basket

bed

path

Note: Reproduce this page for each student. Use the directions on page 56 to help students complete the activity.

Sequence the Story

Note: Reproduce this page for each student. Use the directions on page 56 to help students complete the activity.

Little Red Riding Hood Puppets

A Basket of Goodies for Granny

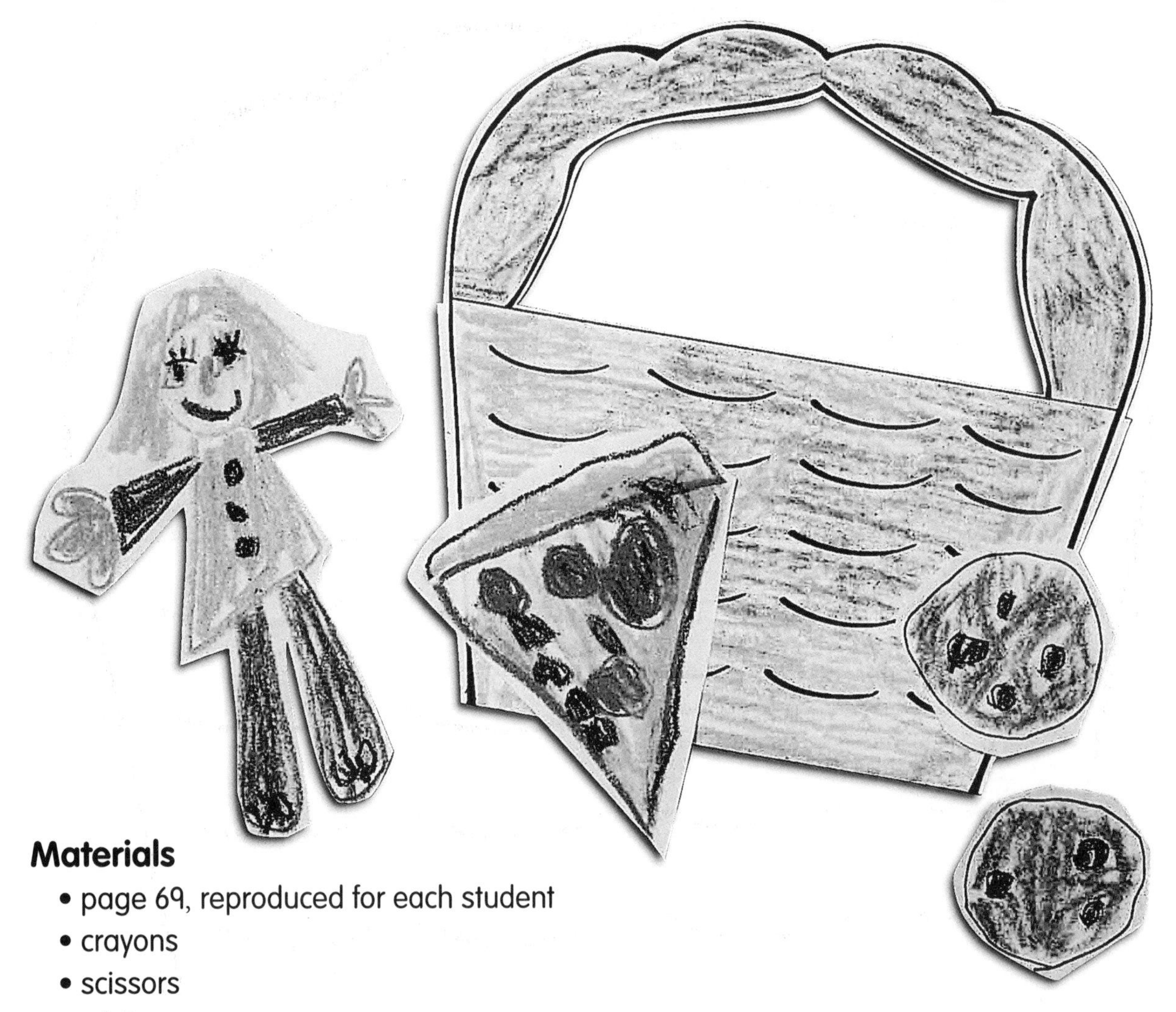

Materials

- page 69, reproduced for each student
- crayons
- scissors
- white scrap paper
- glue

Steps to Follow

1. Have students color and cut out the basket pattern and fold it along the fold line. Then have students glue the basket together around the outer edges.
2. Have students recall the basket of goodies that Little Red Riding Hood took to her grandmother. Have them tell why she brought the goodies.
3. Ask students to guess what was inside the basket. Have them think about what they would bring to a sick grandmother. Invite them to share their ideas.
4. Have students use white scrap paper and crayons to draw the items they would bring to a sick grandmother. Have them cut out the items and glue them in the paper basket.
5. Invite students to share their baskets. Have them identify the items and tell how each one would make a sick grandmother feel better.

Basket Pattern

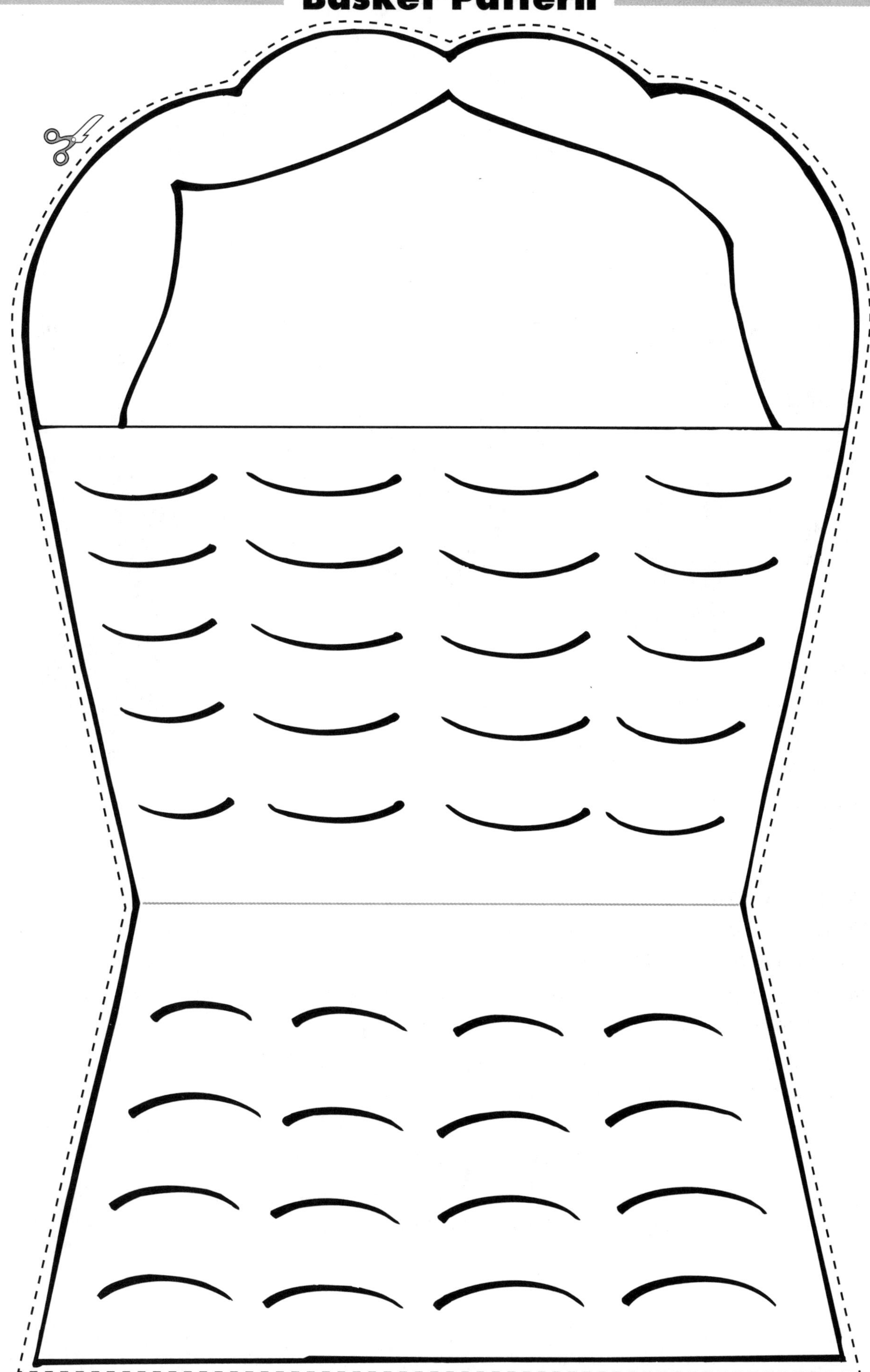

Pocket 6

The Three Billy Goats Gruff

Pocket Label and Bookmark .... page 71
Have students use these reproducibles to make The Three Billy Goats Gruff pocket label and bookmark. (See page 2.)

The Story of
The Three Billy Goats Gruff .... pages 72–76
Share and discuss this story of three hungry goats and the terrible troll who blocked their route to food. Reproduce the story on pages 73–76 for students. Use the teaching ideas on page 72 to preview, read, and review the story. Follow up with the "More to Explore" activities.

The Three Billy Goats Gruff
Word Book .... pages 77 and 78
This minibook helps students understand prepositions as they read words from the story. Have students trace the words, color the pictures, and staple the pages together. After the book is assembled, have students read the words aloud as they point to the matching pictures.

Sequence the Story .... page 79
Have students color and cut out these sequence cards and glue them in order onto a 4" x 18" (10 x 45.5 cm) strip of construction paper. Fold the strip in half to fit it in the pocket.

The Three Billy Goats Gruff
Finger Puppets .... pages 80 and 81
Students will love using these delightful finger puppets to retell the story of "The Three Billy Goats Gruff."

A Terrible Troll .... page 82
Students use paper scraps and their imagination to create their own terrible troll. Extend the activity by having students tell a story about their troll.

The Three Billy Goats Gruff

Story characters:

Little Billy Goat Gruff

Middle Billy Goat Gruff

Big Billy Goat Gruff

Troll

I liked this story:

☐ Yes

☐ No

This bookmark belongs to

____

(your name)

Share The Three Billy Goats Gruff

Preview the Story

State the title of the story, and have students read aloud the names of the characters listed on the bookmark. Distribute copies of the story (pages 73–76), and have students preview the first three pictures. Invite students who are unfamiliar with the story to predict what problem the goats face when crossing the bridge.

Read the Story

Read the story aloud as students follow along. Have students track the text and underline or frame key words. Point out picture clues and context clues that help explain parts of the story. After you have read the story aloud, encourage students to reread the story independently or with a partner.

Review the Story

Discuss the characters, setting, and plot of the story. Ask questions such as the following to help students recall the sequence of events, identify problems and solutions, recognize cause-and-effect relationships, and share opinions:

- Why did the goats want to cross the bridge?
- Why was it dangerous for the goats to cross the bridge?
- Which goat went across the bridge first? Next? Last?
- How did the goats get rid of the troll?
- Who do you think was the bravest goat? Why?
- Would you have gone on the bridge? Why or why not?

More to Explore

- Act Out the Story

  This is a great story for an impromptu play. Set up a table and two chairs to make a bridge. Then select three "Billy Goats Gruff" and a "troll." Encourage students to make up their own dialog as they act out the play. (Set up rules about how to get rid of the troll; no pushing off the table!) Repeat the play until everyone that wants to participate has had an opportunity.

- Sizing Up Words

  Use manipulatives, such as toy animals and building blocks, to help students understand the meanings of these adjectives: *big, bigger, biggest; little, littler, littlest; large, larger, largest; small, smaller, smallest; tall, taller, tallest; wide, wider, widest; long, longer, longest.* Then invite students to use the words to compare and contrast the animals and objects mentioned in the story.

- Compare and Contrast Different Versions

  Read aloud another version of "The Three Billy Goats Gruff." Work with students to compare and contrast the two versions, using a Venn diagram or a comparison chart.

There once was a family of billy goats named Gruff.
The three billy goats lived near a wide river.
On the other side of the river was a big hill covered with tall green grass.

2

"That grass sure looks good!" said Little Billy Goat Gruff.

"It must taste better than our grass," said Middle Billy Goat Gruff.

"Don't go near the bridge," warned Big Billy Goat Gruff. "There's a bad troll living under it. He will eat you."

3

The next day, Little Billy Goat Gruff was hungry. He just had to get some of that grass! Tip-tap, tip-tap went his little hooves as he started to cross the bridge.

Out jumped the troll. "I'm going to eat you up!" he growled.

"Oh no!" begged Little Billy Goat Gruff. "Why don't you wait for my brother? He is much bigger and tastier than me."

"Okay, you can go," said the troll.

4

Soon Middle Billy Goat Gruff showed up.
Clip-clop, clip-clop went his hooves as he started to cross the bridge.

Out jumped the troll. "I'm going to eat you up!" he growled.

"Oh no!" begged Middle Billy Goat Gruff. "Why don't you wait for my brother? He is much bigger and tastier than me."

"Okay, you can go," said the troll.

5

Finally Big Billy Goat Gruff showed up.
Tromp-tramp, tromp-tramp went his hooves as he started to cross the bridge.

Out jumped the troll. "I'm going to eat you up!" he growled.

"Come up and try!" said Big Billy Goat Gruff.

6

Big Billy Goat Gruff saw the troll on the bridge.
He lowered his head and ran after the troll.
He used his horns to throw the troll high into the sky.

The troll was never seen again.

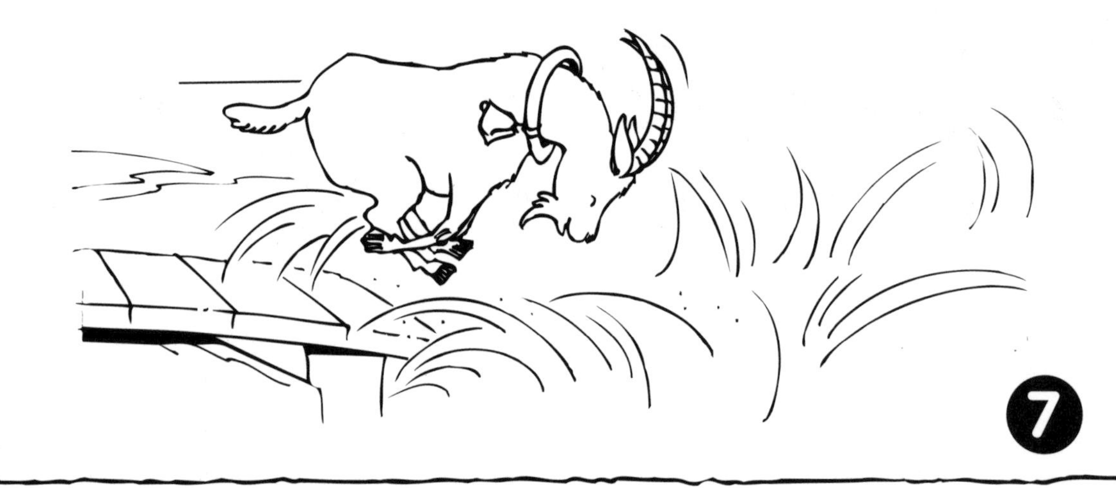

7

The End

8

Note: Reproduce pages 77 and 78 for each student. Use the directions on page 70 to help students complete the activity.

The Three Billy Goats Gruff Word Book

The Three Billy Goats Gruff Word Book

(your name)

goat

troll

The Three Billy Goats Gruff Word Book

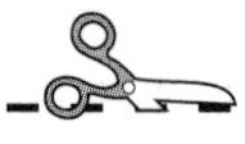

little goat

big goat

on the bridge

under the bridge

one troll

three goats

on the hill

near the hill

Note: Reproduce this page for each student. Use the directions on page 70 to help students complete the activity.

Sequence the Story

The Three Billy Goats Gruff Finger Puppets

Materials

- page 81, reproduced for each student
- crayons
- scissors
- glue
- resealable plastic bag

Steps to Follow

❶ Guide students through the following steps to make the finger puppets:

a. Color and cut out the puppet pieces.

b. Glue the paper strips as shown to make "rings."

glue

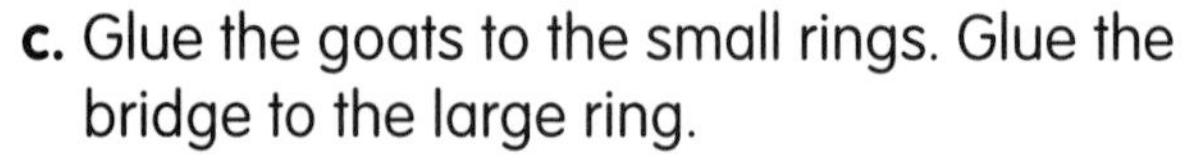

c. Glue the goats to the small rings. Glue the bridge to the large ring.

d. Place the bridge over one hand and the goat puppets on the fingers of the other hand. Hold the bridge puppet in front of the finger puppets while retelling the story.

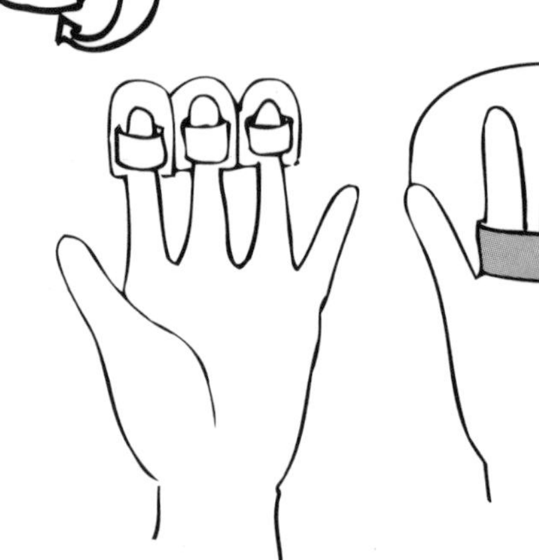

❷ After students use their finger puppets to retell the story, have them put the puppets into a resealable plastic bag and then place the bag in the pocket.

Puppet Patterns

A Terrible Troll

Materials

- 6″ x 9″ (15 x 23 cm) construction paper
- multicolored scraps of construction paper
- scissors
- glue

Steps to Follow

1. Ask students to describe the troll from the story. Discuss why the goats were scared of him.
2. Have students make their own scary trolls. Demonstrate how to cut the corners off a sheet of construction paper to make the troll's rounded head. Have students use scraps of paper to add the eyes, nose, mouth, and any other features they choose (ears, eyebrows, hair, and so on).

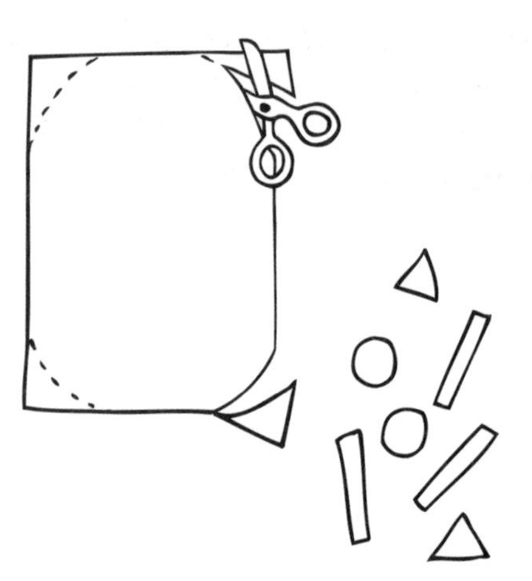

3. Display the trolls on a bulletin board for everyone to see. Have students compare and contrast the pictures.
4. When the display comes down, put the trolls into students' pockets.

Too Much Noise

Pocket Label and Bookmark .... page 84
Have students use these reproducibles to make the Too Much Noise pocket label and bookmark. (See page 2.)

The Story of Too Much Noise .... pages 85–89
Share and discuss this story about a frustrated mother who can't work in her noisy house. Reproduce the story on pages 86–89 for students. Use the teaching ideas on page 85 to preview, read, and review the story. Follow up with the "More to Explore" activities.

In the Noisy House .... pages 90 and 91
Students will love reading this miniature house of words from the story. Have students color, cut out, and staple the pages to make the book.

Sequence the Story .... page 92
Have students color and cut out these sequence cards and glue them in order onto a 4" x 18" (10 x 45.5 cm) strip of construction paper. Fold the strip in half to fit it in the pocket.

Too Much Noise Storyboard...... pages 93 and 94
Students move characters in and out of a storyboard house as they retell the story. Extend the activity by having students add more noisy things to the house.

Too Much Noise

Story characters:

Mother

Father

Grandpa

Baby

Children

Dog

Cat

Rooster

Cow

I liked this story:

☐ Yes

☐ No

This bookmark belongs to

____

(your name)

Share Too Much Noise

Preview the Story

State the title of the story, and have students read aloud the names of the characters listed on the bookmark. Distribute copies of the story (pages 86–89), and have students preview the first picture. Invite students who are unfamiliar with the story to predict why the woman is unhappy and guess what she does to solve her problem.

Read the Story

Read the story aloud as students follow along. Have students track the text and underline or frame key words. Point out picture clues and context clues that help explain parts of the story. After you have read the story aloud, encourage students to reread the story independently or with a partner.

Review the Story

Discuss the characters, setting, and plot of the story. Ask questions such as the following to help students recall the sequence of events, identify problems and solutions, and draw conclusions:

- Why was the mother unhappy?
- Where did she go for help?
- What did the grandpa tell her to do first? Next? Last?
- Why do you think the mother thought the house was quiet after she took the animals back outside?
- What would you have done to make the house quieter?

More to Explore

- Opposites

  Explain what opposites are by using the words *noisy* and *quiet* as examples. Then give a word and ask students to say a word that is the opposite. Use simple examples, such as *hot/cold*, *big/little*, and *fast/slow*. Use more difficult words for more advanced students.

- Sound Off

  Review with students the sounds that the characters make in the story. Then reread the story aloud, but instead of reading the action words in the refrain, point to students and have them make the sounds. (You may choose to read the word *yelling* to avoid excessive noise in the classroom.)

- Compare and Contrast Different Versions

  Read aloud another version of "Too Much Noise." Work with students to compare and contrast the two versions, using a Venn diagram or a comparison chart.

The children were yelling.
The baby was crying.
Father was pounding.
Mother was sighing.

“I can’t do my work,” Mother said.
“This crowd is much too loud!”

Mother went to see Grandpa. "Grandpa, my house is too loud. The children are yelling. The baby is crying. Father is pounding. There is too much noise. What can I do?"

Grandpa looked up. "No problem," he said. "Bring the dog and the cat into the house."

Mother walked home and called the dog and the cat into the house.

3

Soon...

The dog was barking.
Cat fur was flying.

The children were yelling.
The baby was crying.
Father was pounding.
Mother was sighing.

"I can't do my work," Mother said.
"This crowd is much too loud!"

4

Mother went back to Grandpa. “Grandpa, my house is much noisier. The children are still yelling. The baby is still crying. Father is still pounding. And now the dog is barking at the cat. What can I do?”

Grandpa nodded. “No problem,” he said.

“Bring the rooster and the cow into the house.”

Mother walked home. She pulled the cow and the rooster into the house.

5

Soon...

The cow was mooing;
The rooster replying.
The dog was barking.
Cat fur was flying.

The children were yelling.
The baby was crying.
Father was pounding.
Mother was sighing.

“I can’t do my work,” Mother said.
“This crowd is much too loud!”

6

Mother went back to Grandpa. "Grandpa, my house is even noisier. The children are still yelling. The baby is still crying. Father is still pounding. The dog is still barking at the cat. And now the cow is mooing and the rooster is crowing. What can I do?"

Grandpa smiled. "No problem," he said. "The cat and the dog and the cow and the rooster must go back outside."

7

Mother walked back home. She took the cow, the rooster, the cat, and the dog outside. The children were still yelling. The baby was still crying. Father was still pounding. Mother smiled. "Now I can do my work! The house is so quiet."

8

Note: Reproduce pages 90 and 91 for each student. Use the directions on page 83 to help students complete the activity.

In the Noisy House

In the Noisy House

____

(your name)

Father

baby

children

In the Noisy House

Note: Reproduce this page for each student. Use the directions on page 83 to help students complete the activity.

Sequence the Story

Too Much Noise Storyboard

Materials

- page 94, reproduced for each student
- 9" x 12" (23 x 30.5 cm) sheets of construction paper
- stapler
- crayon
- scissors
- glue

Steps to Follow

1. Make a paper pocket for each student. Fold up the bottom of the construction paper about 3" (7.5 cm) and staple the sides.
2. Distribute the reproduced sheets. Have students color and cut out the animals and the mother. Have them store the cutouts in the paper pocket until needed.
3. Guide students as they color and cut out the two houses (the main house and Grandpa's house) and glue them onto the construction paper as shown.
4. Invite students to use their storyboards as you read the story aloud. Students move the mother back and forth between her house and Grandpa's house as she goes for advice. They move the animals in and out of the lower windows to indicate what is happening in the story.
5. Encourage students to use their storyboards to retell the story to a partner.
6. Extend the activity by discussing other noisy things that could be included in the house. Have students draw a noisy object and write or dictate a sentence about it.

Too Much Noise Storyboard

Note: Use this evaluation activity after students have completed their Folktales and Fairy Tales book.

Name: ________________________________

Folktales and Fairy Tales Evaluation

My favorite folktale or fairy tale is ____________________.

I like it best because ________________________________

____

____.

This is my favorite character:

Note: Use this evaluation activity after students have completed their Folktales and Fairy Tales book.

Name: ______________________________

Folktale and Fairy Tale Characters

Circle the make-believe things.